Peboan and Seegwun

Peboan and Seegwun

RETOLD AND ILLUSTRATED BY

CHARLES LARRY

FARRAR, STRAUS AND GIROUX

NEW YORK

At the end of winter, an old man sat alone in his lodge. Day after day, he heard nothing but the howling wind sweeping snow across the land.

One night, as the lodge fire was dying, a young man peeked through the door. With cheeks flushed, eyes sparkling like sunlight on water, he greeted the old man with a smile.

"Ah, my son," said the old man, motioning for his visitor to sit. "I am happy to see you." He filled a carved pipe with kinnikinnick, a mixture of willow bark and tobacco. After lighting the pipe, he handed it to the young man to smoke. Then they each spoke in turn.

"When I blow my breath," the old man said, "streams stand still—water becomes stiff and hard as quartz."

"I breathe," said the young man, "and flowers spring up everywhere."

"When I toss my hair," said the old man, "leaves fall from the trees and birds fly to distant lands. With my breath, the ground freezes hard as flint and snow covers the world, while the animals hide."

 "I shake my hair," said the young man, "and rain falls upon the earth, causing plants to grow. My voice recalls the birds. My breath unlocks the streams, which fill the air with musical laughter."

As the sun rose, warming the place, the old man became silent. A robin and bluebird began to sing as the breeze carried the fragrance of herbs and flowers.

Daylight revealed to Seegwun, the Spirit of Spring, the true nature of his host. Looking at the old man, he saw the icy face of Peboan, Old Man Winter. Streams began to flow from Peboan's eyes. As the sun climbed higher and higher, Peboan grew less and less and finally melted completely away.

Where his lodge fire had been, there appeared a spring beauty, one of the earliest to bloom of the northern flowers.

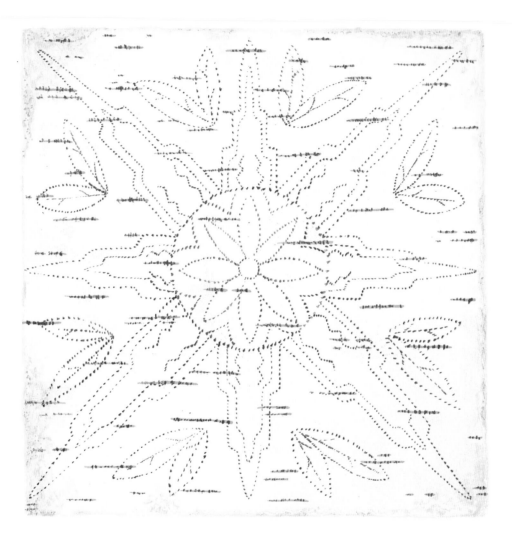

A NOTE

The story of Peboan (Pe-BONE) and Seegwun (See-GWUN) was collected from the Ojibwa by Henry Schoolcraft and included in a book called *Algic Researches* published in 1839. The Ojibwa tell several versions of the story portraying the transition from winter to spring. In this one, the transition is relatively gentle. In other versions, it is not.

The Ojibwa are a northern forest people who migrated from eastern North America before settling in what are now the states of Michigan, Wisconsin, and Minnesota. They did not call themselves Ojibwa, a name of uncertain meaning given to them by others. Their own name for themselves, Anishinabe, means "One of the People."

The Anishinabe learned to live with the land. They knew how to use the things of the forest for their homes, clothing, tools, weapons, food, and medicine. In this story I have shown the daily life of the Anishinabe in the seasons of spring and winter (and, in one instance, fall). Some of the activities depicted are ice fishing for sturgeon, canoe making, bear hunting, and the gathering, processing, and storing of wild rice. Other scenes focus on the animal and plant life found in the North Woods.

I have tried to show how the Anishinabe lived before they had any contact with European peoples. Therefore, you will not find metal tools or weapons, kettles, or cloth. As the scenes here depict the Anishinabe in their daily activities, you will not see much of the beautiful porcupine quill work for which these people are well known. Elaborately decorated clothing was probably used for ceremonial or festive occasions only.

I hope I may be forgiven for having taken poetic liberties when sources were vague or even contradictory. For any mistakes, I apologize to the Anishinabe.

I would like to thank all the people, past and present, at the University Libraries, Northern Illinois University, who stood behind me on this project.

And a big thank you to Emmylou.   C.L.

For Nancy, who opened the door
and Stephen, who let me in

Copyright © 1993 by Charles Larry
All rights reserved
Published simultaneously in Canada by HarperCollins*CanadaLtd*
Color separations by Vimnice
Printed and bound in the United States of America
by Worzalla
Designed by Lilian Rosenstreich
First edition, 1993

Library of Congress Cataloging-in-Publication Data

Larry, Charles.
     Peboan and Seegwun / retold and illustrated by Charles Larry.—1st ed.
        p.   cm.
     Summary: An encounter between Peboan, Old Man Winter, and
Seegwun, the Spirit of Spring, marks the transition from one season to
another.
     1. Ojibwa Indians—Legends. 2. Seasons—Folklore. [1. Ojibwa
Indians—Legends. 2. Indians of North America—Legends.
3. Seasons—Folklore] I. Title.
E99.C6C43   1993   398.2′089973—dc20   93-10092   CIP   AC